The Good Neighbors' CHEESE FEAST

A Cheesy Mouse Tale of Subtraction with Regrouping

Written by Mark Ramsay • Illustrated by Susan G. Robinson

STRATEGIC
Educational Tools

For my children:
Mark, Adam, and Jenna,
with love and thanks.
- MR

For my parents, who supported
my every artistic whim.
- SR

Published by
Strategic Educational Tools
293 Center Street
East Aurora, New York 14052
www.strategicedtools.com

Text © 2009 by Mark Ramsay
Illustrations © 2009 by Susan G. Robinson

Book design and cover by Susan G. Robinson.
Edited by Nancy Raines Day.

Printed in the United States of America.
First Edition

Publisher's Cataloging-in-Publication data

Ramsay, Mark, 1968-
The good neighbors' cheese feast - a cheesy mouse tale of subtraction with
regrouping / written by Mark Ramsay ; illustrated by Susan G. Robinson.
p. cm.
Series : The good neighbors math series
Summary : The good neighbors use what they know about subtraction with
regrouping, the base-ten number system, base-ten blocks, and place value to
divide their cheese so that each of them can make a recipe.

ISBN 978-0-9842863-1-7 [1. Mathematics --Fiction. 2. Arithmetic--Fiction.
3. Subtraction--Fiction.] I. Robinson, Susan Gail. II. Title.

PZ7.R145 Go 2010
[E]—dc22   2009910460

Hello, my neighbors call me Onesie.

I guess it's because I wear a one-piece outfit
with my favorite number on the front.

I live next-door to Tenor.
He *loves* to sing in his high-pitched voice.

Tenor lives next-door to Hund-Red,
the most glowing and generous mouse you will ever meet.

We all love cheese - no matter what its size!

I eat small cheese cubes,
the same cubes that make up
the bigger pieces of cheese.

Tenor eats medium-sized cheese sticks...

...made of ten cubes.

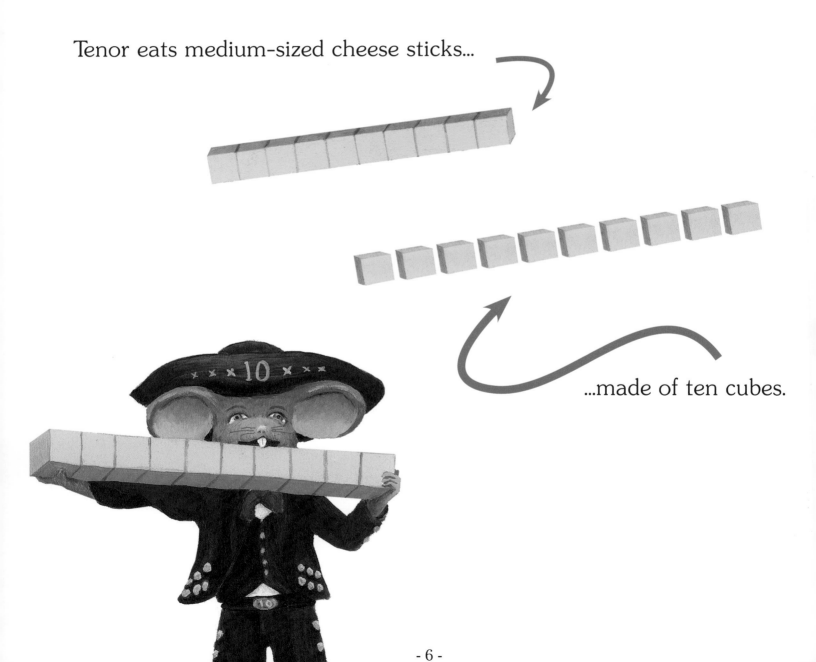

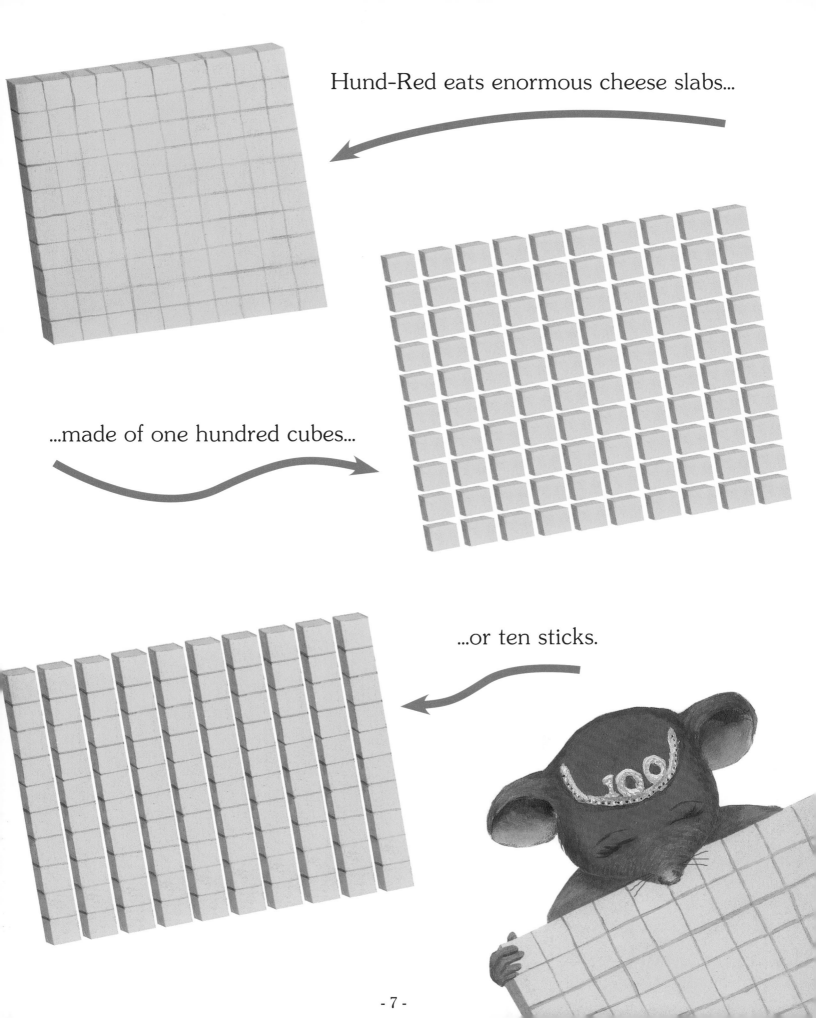

Hund-Red eats enormous cheese slabs...

...made of one hundred cubes...

...or ten sticks.

Every Monday morning, we rush to the cheese factory
to stock up on cheese.

We can each store up to nine pieces of our favorite size of cheese,
so we buy the amount we need to fill up our homes.

10

CHEESE STICKS

1

CHEESE CUBES

WELCOME

When all three of our houses are full of cheese,
how many **cubes** would that make altogether?
Look back at pages 4 and 5 if you need a hint.

Even though we each
buy and store our own cheese...

we believe that it
belongs to all of us.

Our motto is,
Mi queso es su queso (mee KAY-so es soo KAY-so),
which means *My cheese is your cheese* in Spanish.

Now that you know all about my two neighbors and me,
let me tell you about our cheese feast.

On Saturday morning, after five days of cheese eating,
Hund-Red, Tenor and I met to spruce up
our Good Neighbor Award.

"Too bad we didn't celebrate last week, when we received the award. Storing all the cheese the mayor gave us really wiped us out!" I said.

"It's never too late to celebrate," replied Hund-Red. "Let's have a cheese feast!"

"Tonight, tonight!" piped Tenor.

So we planned for the feast.

Then we all returned home to look for our favorite recipes
and begin making our cheesy dishes.

How much cheese did each of us have to cook and bake with?
*How many **cubes** would that make altogether?*

My cheese soup recipe called for five cheese cubes,
but I only had three!

CHEESE SOUP

Can you guess what I did?

Tenor looked at my empty cart, then looked at me.

"Uh-oh!" sang Tenor. "Cheese shortage, *amigo*? Take one of my five sticks. *Mi queso es su queso!*"

"*Gracias*, but will you have enough for your macaroni and cheese?" I asked.

"I can't find my recipe, and I've looked *everywhere*!" sang Tenor. "But I *think* four sticks will be enough."

Once home, I began slicing Tenor's stick into cubes.

Do you know how many cubes I sliced? How many cubes did I have altogether?

I didn't have room for all thirteen cubes inside, so I briefly kept the ten freshly sliced cubes outside while I prepared to make my soup.

I cast five cubes into my soup pot.

How many cubes did I have left?

While my soup simmered on the stove, I stored my eight leftover cubes inside.

Tenor finally found his macaroni and cheese recipe. It called for eight cheese sticks, but he only had four!

Can you guess what Tenor did?

Hund-Red looked at Tenor's empty cart, then looked at him.

"Oh, you poor thing!" said Hund-Red. "You must have one of my seven slabs. *Mi queso es su queso!*"

"*Gracias*, but will you have enough for your cheesecake?" sang Tenor.

"I've been *so* busy helping others that I haven't peeked at my recipe yet, but I *hope* six slabs will be enough," answered Hund-Red.

Once home, Tenor began slicing Hund-Red's slab into sticks.

Do you know how many sticks Tenor sliced?
How many sticks did he have altogether?

enor didn't have room for all fourteen sticks inside, so he briefly kept the ten eshly sliced sticks outside while he prepared to make his macaroni and cheese.

Tenor stirred eight sticks together with the macaroni noodles.

How many sticks did Tenor have left?

While Tenor's macaroni melted in the microwave, he moved his six leftover sticks inside.

Hund-Red finally studied her cheesecake recipe. "Phew! Six slabs *is* enough," she said.

CHEESECAKE

She slopped four slabs into the cheesecake batter.

How many slabs did Hund-Red have left?

While Hund-Red's cheesecake cooled on the counter, she caught some Zs because her two leftover slabs were already safely inside.

We did it.
We each made our feast food with cheese to spare!

How many **cubes** would our leftover cheese make?

Saturday evening we met outside for the feast.

We began with my cheese soup.

What a light and dainty taste!

Hund-Red
(Slabs)

Cheese from neighbor

plus +

Cheese before making dish

minus -

Cheese used in dish

equals =

Leftover cheese

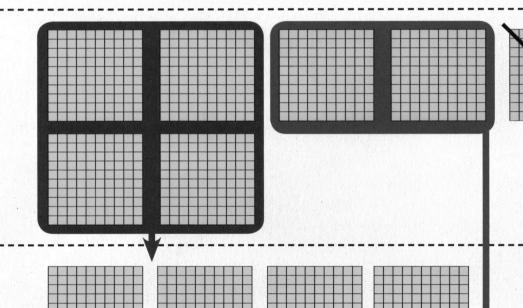

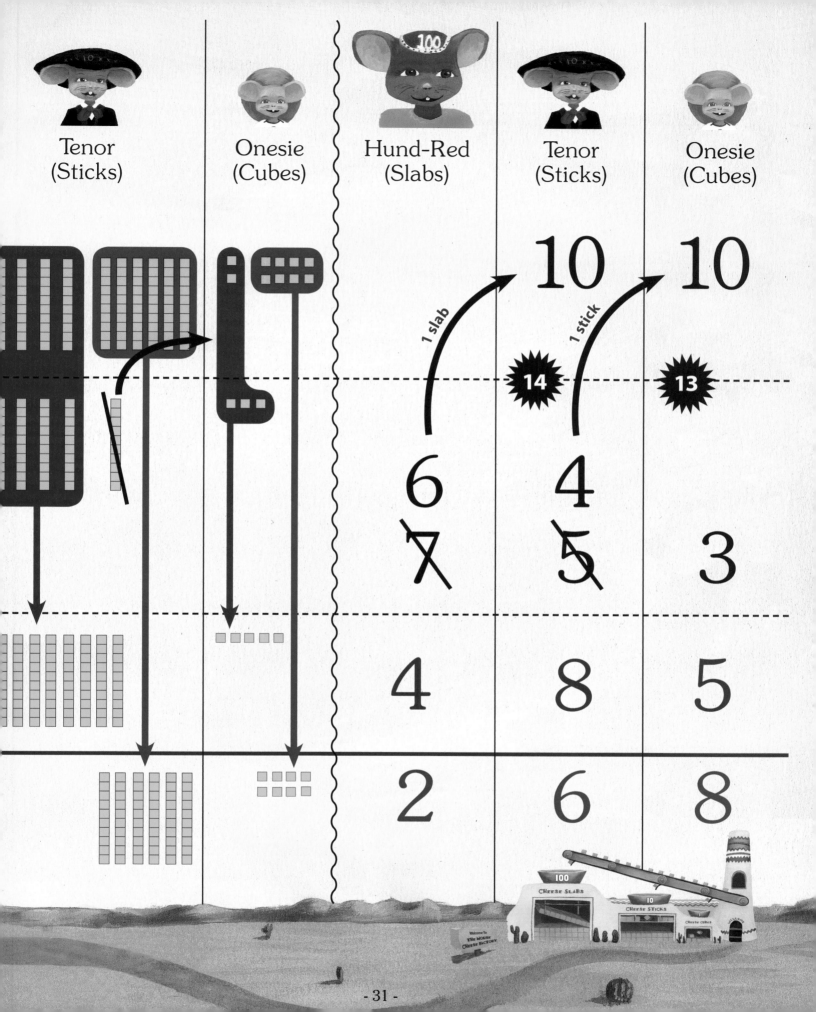

Tenor (Sticks)	Onesie (Cubes)	Hund-Red (Slabs)	Tenor (Sticks)	Onesie (Cubes)
			10	10
		6	4	
		7̶	5̶	3
		4	8	5
		2	6	8

1 slab

1 stick

14

13

The Good Neighbors Math Series

The Good Neighbors Store an Award -
A Cheesy Mouse Tale of Addition with Regrouping

When The Good Neighbors each receive a cheesy award, some of the mice discover that they do not have enough room to store it all safely inside their houses. Can The Good Neighbors work together to solve their cheese storage problem? The mice's story models the addition with regrouping process as demonstrated with base-ten blocks.

The Good Neighbors' Cheese Feast -
A Cheesy Mouse Tale of Subtraction with Regrouping

When The Good Neighbors decide to have a cheese feast, some of the mice discover that they do not have enough cheese to make their cheesy dishes. Can The Good Neighbors work together to solve their cheese shortage problem? The mice's story models the subtraction with regrouping process as demonstrated with base-ten blocks.

Look for new books and accessories coming soon!

Visit *The Good Neighbors Math Series* at www.strategicedtools.com!

- Purchase books and accessories
- Download free activity sheets
- Receive instructional ideas and tips